Illustrated by

Laura Hughes

We're going on an EGG HUNT

BLOOMSBURY
LONDON OXFORD NEW YORK NEW DELHI SYDNEY

We're going on an egg hunt.
We're going to find them all.
We're REALLY excited . . .

HOORAY for
Easter Day!

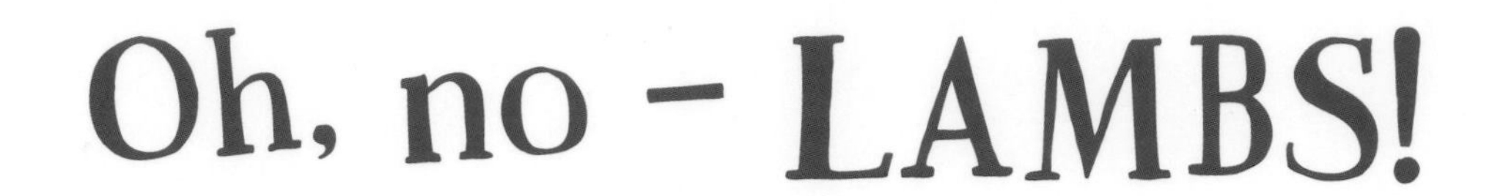

Oh, no – LAMBS!

Can't go over them.

Can't go under them.

Can't go around them.

Got to go through them . . .
Baa!
Baa!
Baa!

We're going on an egg hunt.
We're going to find them all.
We're REALLY excited . . .

HOORAY for
Easter Day!
milk

Oh, no – CHICKS!

Can't go over them.

Can't go under them.

Can't go around them.

Got to go through them . . .
Cheep!
Cheep!
Cheep!

We're going on an egg hunt.
We're going to find them all.
We're REALLY excited . . .

HOORAY for
Easter Day!

Oh, no – BEES!

Can't go over them.

Can't go under them.

Can't go around them.

Got to go through them . . .
Buzz!
Buzz!
Buzz!

We're going on an egg hunt.
We're going to find them all.
We're REALLY excited . . .

HOORAY for
Easter Day!

Oh, no – DUCKS!

Can't go over them.

Can't go under them.

Can't go around them.

Got to go through them . . .
Quack!
Quack!
Quack!

We're going on an egg hunt.
We've found this VERY BIG one . . .
We're **really** excited.

HOORAY for
Easter Day!

Back through the ducks.

Quack!
Quack!
Quack!

Back through the bees.

Back through the chicks.

Back through the lambs.

AND . . .

HOORAY!
It's Easter eggs
for TEA!

For Sani Wolf and Till Wolf

Bloomsbury Publishing, London, Oxford, New York, New Delhi and Sydney

First published in Great Britain in 2016 by Bloomsbury Publishing Plc
50 Bedford Square, London WC1B 3DP

www.bloomsbury.com

BLOOMSBURY is a registered trademark of Bloomsbury Publishing Plc

A CIP catalogue record of this book is available from the British Library

ISBN 978 1 4088 7386 1 (HB)
5 7 9 10 8 6 4

ISBN 978 1 4088 7011 2 (PB)
3 5 7 9 10 8 6 4

All papers used by Bloomsbury Publishing are natural, recyclable products made from wood grown in well managed forests. The manufacturing processes conform to the environmental regulations of the country of origin

Printed in China by Leo Paper Products, Heshan, Guangdong